Published by Stark Raving Graphics Bainbridge, NY 13733
1 607 229-9405

Printed in the USA

To my Mom and Pop
For their love and support

Many thanks to the many people who help make
my world a wonderful place:

John H. Ott, Hank Roberts and his family. Birtie, Guido and the wee Harpo, The Dawson gang and all the distinguished competition at the Afton Golf Club. Innisbrooke, Jill at Plainsmen Gallery, Upper Catskill Council on the Arts, Chenango Arts Council, Colorscapes, Wendy and Andy, Grassroots, Autumn Cafe, Barb, Mark and the mad scientists at Golden Artist Colors. Sophie and Bernie, Daniel Tenent, T-Bone, Jerry D. and the Dog.

A very special thank you to Michael Gordon at Triumphant, my old buddy Eric Wilson at U.S.A. Custom Pad and my brother Jeffery Price and his camera work in getting this thing out on the street.

"And please consider this, none of us needs huge amounts of money to live an abundant life and to be happy. A backyard solar barbaque with family and friends, what could be better!!!"

- Hank Roberts

Hank and Frank were up early.

They were racing sticks in the stream that ran through the Many Mile Marsh. While they did this, the sunrise cut through the morning mists and started another beautiful day in the Rockabout Hills.

The two lizards were on the way to their friend's house. Soon the Willow Rill Mill where Dr. Croaker lived came into view. "Hurry up Frank" Hank called back to his brother. "It's just a bit further".

Sun and Moon
! ALL STARS !
SATURDAY ALL DAY

Dr. Croaker was also up early. "Why aren't you boys in school?" Asked the kind old blue frog. "We wanted to listen to you and the Allstars rehearse" said Hank. "Besides, it's Saturday", added Frank. "Very well then, and after that you can help us put up the posters I'm printing. We're having a show this weekend!"

Doctor Croaker was a frog of many talents. Not only was he an excellent artist, he was the leader of the greatest band in all the land. The Sun and Moon Allstars. Everyone loved to listen to Dr. Croaker and the elfin Musicians.

On their way back from the rehearsal Hank and Frank met Mrs. Mouse and her son Mitchell. Mrs. Mouse was miffed because she was behind with her washing. She said there was something foul in the water. They asked if Mitchell could help put up posters. Mrs. Mouse said "She was sorry but Mitchell had chores of his own at the cheese shop."

With that the lizards decided to split up so they could cover more ground. Hank took the west marsh trail since it was longer and he was faster. He also didn't want his little brother to get lost. Frank went back the way they had come along the east marsh trail, promoting the show along the way.

At the far end of the pond Hank came upon some wood fairies. They were looking at an old drain pipe. It hadn't worked in a long time but it was working now and the fairies were not happy at all. "It smells like rotten vegetables", said Hank. "We'll soon put a stop to this" replied the fairie queen. The madder she got the more she sparkled. Soon she disappeared and there was only the sound of rustling leaves.

By the time Hank returned to town Frank had already hung up posters. Everyone knew about the show but something else was on their minds. They were miffed just like Mrs. Mouse. In fact everyone was hoppin' mad because the pond was getting polluted! When Hank mentioned the drain pipe they got even madder. Then someone said I'll bet it's Big Boss Toad!

Boss Toad was a big deal in a small town, or so he thought. He was very proud of his fancy suit, shiny shoes, fine hat and his gold cuff links with the "T" for toad. He had a little business making his Swamp Root Extract. It was actually pretty tasty and very good for you. He sold a fair amount of it and had recently built a bigger extractor. The boss was having a great day until he heard about the show, for he was a jealous toad. "Every one likes that frog more than me, with his music and his Croaker Cola!" "I'll show them." He bellowed. "I'll make so much Swamp Root Tonic I'll be able to give it away. Then everyone will like me!" I've got to put an end to the music show this weekend. "Pondscum, get me Pondscum" he roared.

Slythy Pondscum was the laziest character in all the hills. Sometimes he acted as the sheriff or did dirty work for Boss Toad. Mostly he laid around in the sun, sleeping or fishing. That day he was doing all three. While the pond folk were looking for Boss Toad he was looking for Pondscum and it was some time before the toad found him and shared his plans.

That night out in the woods the fairies had plans of their own. It started with a rustling of leaves and the Fairie Queen appeared. Then the rustling grew louder as the Queen brought forth a terrific storm.

Luckily, most everyone was asleep

for it was a ferocious storm that

seemed to stay in one place and

blew all night long.

By morning, the storm had passed and it was another beautiful day just like always. The storm had done its job and the fairies checked out the smashed drain pipe of Toad's Swamp Root Extractor.

Boss Toad knew nothing of this.

He was up early picking vegetables

as fast as he could. This would be

the biggest batch of Swamp Root

Tonic ever, he thought and smiled

to himself.

When he finished, the wheel barrel was so full he could barely push it. There was all kinds of good stuff, tomatoes, celery, carrots, peppers, onions, and his favorite, turnips, parsnips and rutabagas!

He dumped everything into the machine, turned the dial to full blast and stood back to watch. The extractor rumbled and grumbled, hissed and spit, grunted and groaned. All in all it was running fine.

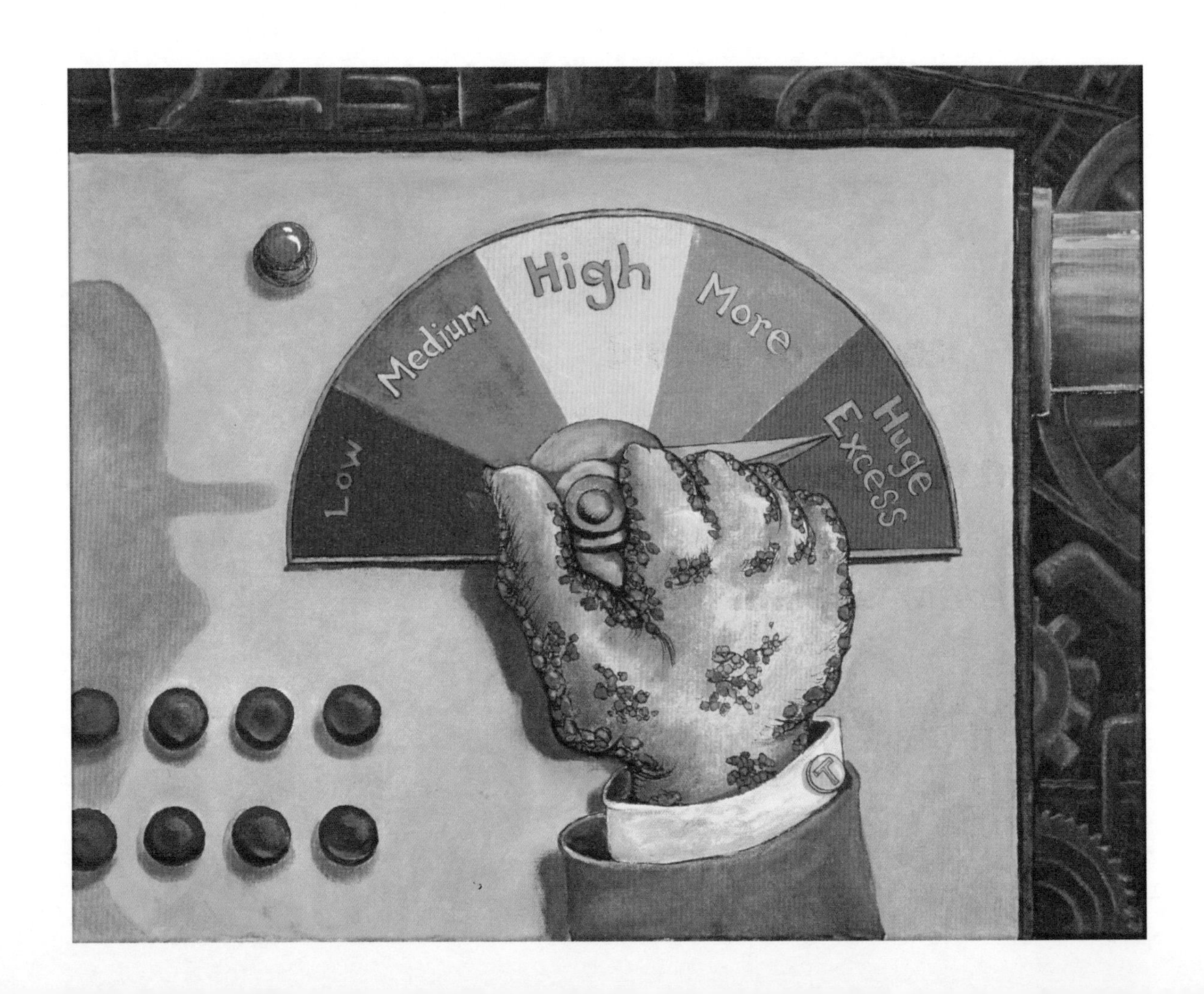

Unfortunately the drain pipe was not working. As it filled with the vegetable waste it began to hiss, and glow, groan and grow. There was a horrible sound, then a huge blast.

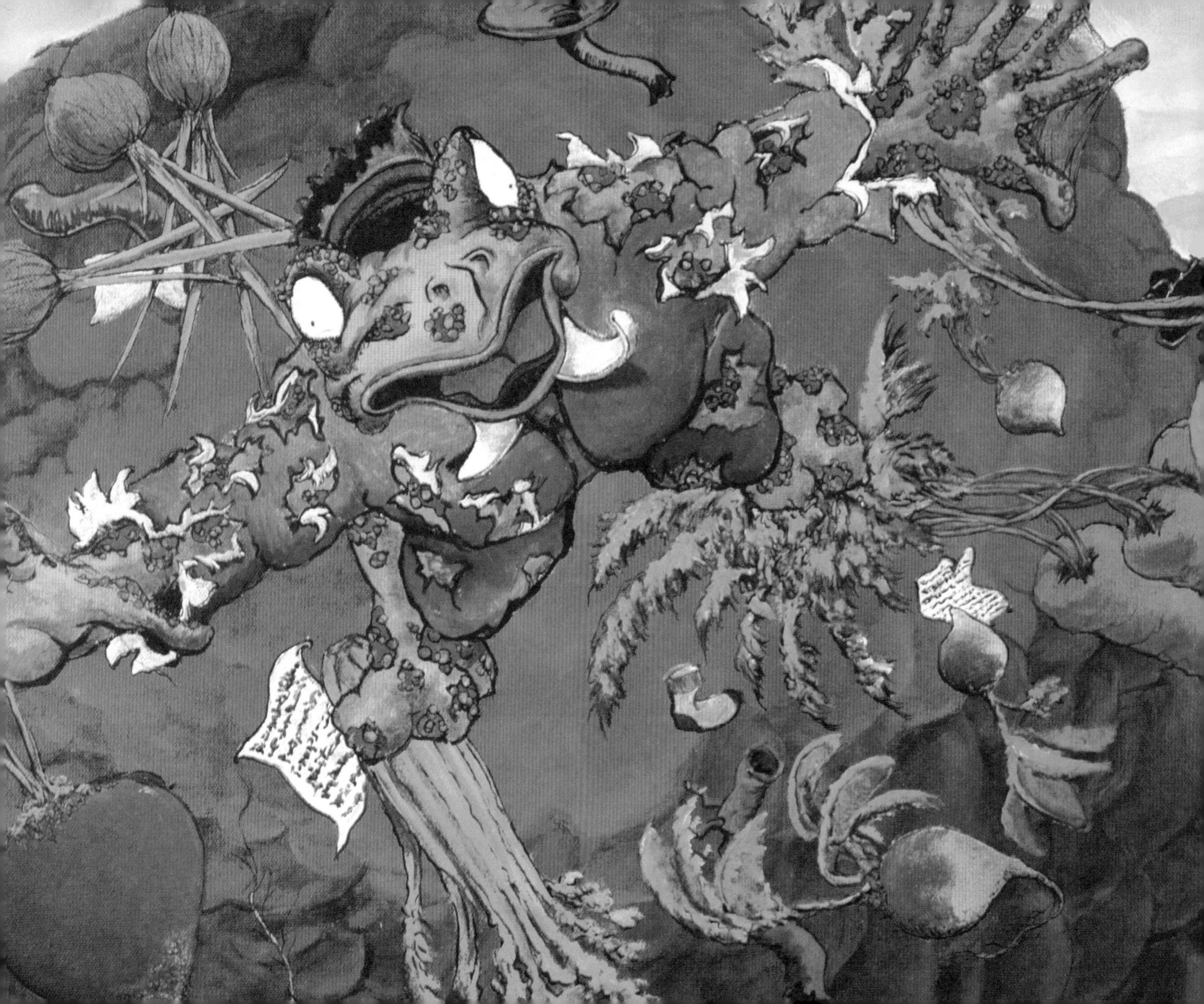

Big Boss Toad was blown high into the sky and all the way to the other end of the pond as well.

Where he landed, ker-splat,

in the middle of a lily pad.

When he came to his senses

he couldn't believe he was still

alive. Toad looked around

and realized he wasn't alone

and he wasn't out of trouble

yet either.

Looking down on the blasted toad were Boss Bass and the viscous Ike the Pike. They too were hoppin' mad. Boss Bass spoke "Look mate, we'll make this short because we're fish we can't stand here all day". "We don't care what you folks on land do as long as it doesn't affect us. But when it affects us here in the water it hurts everyone on land too". "So, if you don't promise to stop polluting the pond you won't make it back to land. For although I do not have a taste for toad, my friend Ike here does."

It was an easy promise for toad to make since his extractor was gone. Gone too were his fancy suit, fine hat, the shiny shoes and the gold cuff links that said "T" for toad. He was a broken toad. Yet he was actually relieved in a strange way. Now he didn't have to be the big deal and the shiny shoes had always been too small. They hurt his feet and made him grumpy all the time. As he made his way home he realized he didn't need any of that fancy stuff at all. The more he thought about it the better he felt. For the first time in a long time the toad was truly **happy!**

When he got back home he told everyone he was sorry for the mess and promised not to pollute the pond anymore. Some of the folks helped him straighten up his shack. The toad was changed and they could see it. Toad was so happy he began to sing. Dr. Croaker and the others couldn't believe their ears. It sounded so good Croaker asked him to sing with the Sun & Moon Allstars which was all the Toad secretly ever wanted anyway.

And so it was, that weekend when the Allstars took the stage, there was Toad front and center singing a song of joy with all his heart. The people loved him. Toad had changed his attitude and the world had changed around him. He didn't need the fancy suit, the fine hat, the stupid small shiny shoes or the gold cuff links that said "T" for Toad. He had everything he ever wanted. Friends he loved and who loved him too.